Coins & Coffins (1962)
Four Young Lady Poets (1962)
Discrepancies and Apparitions (1966)
The George Washington Poems (1967)
Greed: Parts 1 & 2 (1968)
The Diamond Merchant (1968)
Inside the Blood Factory (1968)
Thanking My Mother for Piano Lessons (1969)
The Lament of the Lady Bank Dick (1969)
Greed: Parts 3 & 4 (1969)
The Moon Has a Complicated Geography (1969)
Black Dream Ditty (1970)
The Magellanic Clouds (1970)
Greed: Parts 5-7 (1971)
On Barbara's Shore (1971)
The Motorcycle Betrayal Poems (1971)
Form Is an Extension of Content (1972)
Smudging (1972)
The Pumpkin Pie (1972)
Greed: Parts 8, 9 & 11 (1973)
Dancing on the Grave of a Son of a Bitch (1973)
Looking for the King of Spain (1974)
Trilogy: Coins & Coffins, Discrepancies and
    Apparitions, The George Washington Poems (1974)
The Fable of the Lion and the Unicorn (1975)
Creating a Personal Mythology (1975)
The Wandering Tattler (1975)
Virtuoso Literature for Two and Four Hands (1975)
Variations on a Theme (1976)
Waiting for the King of Spain (1976)
Pachelbel's Canon (1978)
The Man Who Shook Hands (1978)
Trophies (1979)
Cap of Darkness (1980)
Two Poems (1980)
Toward a New Poetry (1980)
The Managed World (1981)
The Magician's Feastletters (1982)

DIANE WAKOSKI

THE MAGICIAN'S FEASTLETTERS

BLACK SPARROW PRESS
SANTA BARBARA –1982

ACKNOWLEDGEMENTS

These poems have appeared or will appear in the named publications: "Breakfast" 1st prize, *Southern Poetry Review,* 1980 contest; "Divers" part of a broadside series published by Barbarian Press; "Coprinus Comatus" *Cedar Rock Review;* "The Boy Magicians" to be a chapbook published by Sheila Webb's new press; "Molokai", *Memphis State Review;* "Making a Sacher Torte," *Blast 3;* "Little Tricks of Linear B", *Ploughshares,* special issue edited by Alan Williamson; "The Ice Queen's Calla Lily Fingers" broadside for poetry reading at the Milwaukee Public Library; "The Dark Procession" *Cumberland Poetry Review;* "Frog Mozart," part of a chapbook published by Red Ozier Press as *The Managed World;* "Orphee" Pomegranate Press anthology; "Leaving Waterloo" Pomegranate Press anthology; "The Frame" to be a broadside published by Sheila Webb; "Whole Sum" *Green River Review;* "Sailor's Daughter" Bisbee Poetry Festival brochure and *Prairie Schooner;* "Peaches" *Prairie Schooner* and broadside published by Toothpaste Press for reading at the Walker Art Museum, February 1981; "For Clint on the Desert" *Tendril;* "Why I Am Not a Painter," *Sulfur #1.*

LIBRARY OF CONGRESS CATALOGING IN PUBLICATION DATA

Wakoski, Diane.
  The magician's feastletters.

  I. Title.
PS3573.A42M33   811'.54   82-1142
ISBN 0-87685-532-X   AACR2
ISBN 0-87685-533-8 (signed cloth ed.)
ISBN 0-87685-531-1 (pbk.)

THE MAGICIAN'S FEASTLETTERS

In Confucian philosophy, unlike Western thought, dis-
cussion of food held a high place in intellectual exchange
as an integral part of living. Confucian scholars, it is said,
found politics too dirty and religion too esoteric.

Elaine Kris, "Yin and Yang Today,"
Petits Propos Culinaires 7

TABLE OF CONTENTS

Autumn

Winter

Spring

Summer

Envoi

AUTUMN

Breakfast

In the Spanish kingdom
of my living room:
the morning sunshine.
A polished wooden table gleams;
silence is the reflection of burnished woods/ pine,
maple, bamboo,
                 waxed to catch the yellow sun.
Outside the wall of windows,
more woods,
these turning to burgundy and gold,
russet,
scarlet,
the wind moving especially
the green leaved ones,
the branches fluttering and bowing,
my courtiers,
my trees.

The kettles boiling now—
            one with water to scald the pot,
            the second with boiling water for the tea.
This morning,
scented Earl Grey,
another courtier, this one perfumed,
a dandy, one of those too-
beautiful men I cannot resist.

On my pine and yellow canvas chair
I rest, drinking the tea,
from a white bone china cup. A remaining crumb
from last night's crusty French bread

is being dazzled on the table's surface/ now
an opal, a pearl, ivory,
a minor jewel dropped from the chest.

In the south window
four sweet basil plants have reached the
height of 18 inches each,
their lime green leaves pungent when
touched/ I give each a little clear water
and pinch off forming bud clusters.

This morning, against all rules,
an egg,
poached in water containing a few drops
of white rice-vinegar, its soft oval body
resting in a poaching cradle of tin,
on three tiny legs, its stiff upright handle
remaining cool
above the boiling white water.

Now, I turn out the egg on a plate
of translucent orange bordered with yellow and black. It
lies there with a vulnerable film over the yolk
while I take my small silver scissors & snip
four large leaves from another basil plant,
this one growing in the kitchen window.
The silver blades slice the leaves in ribbons over
the cooling egg.

Alone, at the big table
with my plate, my single herbed egg, a goblet of
iced water with a fresh sprig of mint,
also from the kitchen window garden,
and my china cup of hot tea, I sit
down

in my morning kingdom.

Everything
we will ever have
is present
in each day's life. There is no more.
Thus, I need
this morning's royalty,
the immortality of the flesh,
the music of wood,
my perfect view of the autumn swamp.

Divers

I am about ready
to leave the Pacific Ocean
with its sandpipers
themselves running swiftly in and out
as the waves do,
and its sound which swishes
immensely in my ears.

I am about ready
to leave the skin diver
in his black rubber suit and big flippers
who walks backwards into the ocean at
Diver's Cove, his footprints
washing out and his black figure
like the one who visited with Emily Dickinson in a
    coach
one day.

I am about ready
to stop remembering the sound of
the tap dance studio down the alley
from our beach house at Laguna
where little girls could be heard
thunking their feet in shining tap shoes
and you dreamed of wearing a black tuxedo
and large tap shoes and dazzling the world
with your twirling, flashing black-shod feet.

I am almost able to forget
the homosexual lovers
we heard moaning in the night

for two weeks while they rented our neighbor's
garage apartment
and their one big fight
which had me trembling under the
heavy maroon comforter
and thinking of the wet beach fog outside
which would make driving dangerous
when one of them leaving would have to get in his
      Porsche
and drive away from the scene.

I surely don't court
disaster, but troubled people come to me,
and I embrace them into my own languidly desperate
life.
The Rider for The Pony Express
has not delivered a letter to me for a decade
yet bad news always finds a way
to me. This face I wear,
a skin-diver's mask.
There is no human voice in the
breathless sea.

Coprinus Comatus:
Evening Mushrooms, Morning Ink

The evening is a straight line,
the red ribbon stretching from the foggy airport
to the wet leaved olive trees,
dripping moisture over
a stamp-pad lawn.

"Look," says my husband,
a tall lumber-jacketed man
pointing to the spot under the olive trees
which I watch all year
for Shaggy Manes.

A little city
of mushrooms, their tall oval white bulbs
pushing out of the grass
barky and scaled
crowds the trees.
"I've been waiting all week
to show you."

He parks the car,
carrying my canvas luggage upstairs
And I breathe the familiar green air
of our apartment
after a week's absence.

Then, putting on rubber-soled shoes and slicker,
I take his hand,
and we go out into the silver evening,
and I fill a basket

with these fresh inky caps, leaving those already
black and deliquescing;
the firm delicate white flesh will
be sautéed in yellow butter
some with fresh tarragon,
others with sweet basil.

I have been away all week,
searching for truth and poetry.
It does not surprise me
to return home
and find a clue to the latter.
The cap of darkness grows on my lawn
under olive trees.

Who says the King of Spain
didn't leave the spore
there?

The Boy Magicians

for Jerome Rothenberg & David Antin,
in friendship

Halloween.
The little bookworm
with her blue plastic glasses
and face pale as cottonmouth's mouth,
loves the day of transformations. Costumed
in a gold satin blouse,
shiny black shorts, and black silky lone-ranger mask
    replacing the
glasses,
big earrings of gold and carmine lipstick,
I was a 6th grade pirate. Feeling
bold, I went to the afternoon magic show
held in the auditorium of Washington Grammar School
in La Habra, California, and sat
in the front row
where I was chosen by Presto The Illusionist
to be levitated.

Without my glasses,
the audience of costumed 6th, 7th, and 8th graders
was blurred,
a tackle-box full of colored and glittering lures,
and my face burned with celebrity. I was a jack-o-lantern
floating up the steps,
the satin black shorts a pool of dark water
reflecting the Aztec torch of my face.

He flattered me,
          "This beautiful girl is going to astound
                    you,"
and I moved my face, the mask glinting and gold earrings
catching the fire,
          "She will float in air
                    with nothing at all to hold her."
Then, he bade me lie on the flat board
which his assistant,
wearing a white strapless top, her breasts bulging
out like water-lily buds, her buttocks packed tightly
into red shorts and flared ballerina skirt,
placed between two chairs.

Flat on the board I lay.
Waving his wand around me in multidirectional circles
he indicated how there could be no invisible wires or
          ropes to hold it.
Then he and his fluffy assistant, one by one, removed
the chairs from beneath the board which held me,
and finally,
they whisked the board itself out
from under my body.

I was flat,
suspended in air, floating.
He passed rings around me
in all directions/
          Magic?

What else?
I was indeed floating.

And then he let me down,
gently.

19

I stood
a bit dazed,
walked around,
and off the stage,
my mask floating in front of my eyes to
the applause of all of Washington School's 6th,
7th, and 8th graders.

To this day,
I do not know
how
I floated/
           perhaps if I'd worn my glasses? Would I have
           seen?
No?

Diane, The Pirate,
in love with blond Jimmy Connor
whose aunt played the piano for auditorium sometimes;
the bookworm who was planning to be a brilliant trial
      lawyer,
or a famous concert pianist,
caught her first fish,
had her first Communion
that day,
when she floated for Presto, The Magician.

* * *

30 Years/
           the giant stands with one foot in the California
                 Pacific,
           one foot in New York's Atlantic:
           what a view they have, upward,
           in the midwest.

20

* * *

While the brown glass bottle of May wine slides around
    in my grocery
bag, held in front of my chest,

                and my purchase,
                    the cast aluminum grill
                    in the shape of a fish,
                    for grilling
                    whole fish,
        wedges
      against me.
I stand in the Saturday afternoon shopping mall,
waiting for The Boy Magicians.
One of them,
in black morning trousers and starched white shirt,
his coat thrown over a chair also holding a black top hat,
a boy as thin as a fishing pole
is restlessly squeezing three soft red balls, turning them
    into
one, or four, or two, or three, again. His face
as white as the fur of the rabbit his friend
soothes and pets in his hands. This boy,
also tall and thin, wears spectacles and a frill-fronted
    dress shirt.
How young they look/ How old they seem/
One constantly soothing the pet rabbit
the other also keeping his hands in constant motion.
Why do they touch me so, in their new but elderly
    clothes?
Why do I want to cry when I see the rabbit in the one
    boy's gentle
but swift hand?

21

In this shopping mall where The Magic Shop is
sponsoring this afternoon of illusion,
and tricks, the audience is small. I, the only one grasping
    my big
shopping bag. Everyone else really came
for the show. A fat boy, with his mother who wears a
    yellow nylon
blouse bulging with hundreds of afternoons of coffee and
    cake, and
double-knit slacks, which would never be handsome,
    even on a movie star,
stands looking out of place. His mother has started a
    conversation
with a 13-year-old, wearing a silvery windbreaker and
    Adidas. Her
questions are clumsy and show her ambition for her son
    and her ig-
norance of magic. The son himself stands there,
    obviously wishing
for an ice cream sundae, seemingly incapable of talking
    for himself
while his mother makes herself sound more and more
    ridiculous. The
pain I feel for fat mother and son embarrasses me. But I
    am res-
cued by the knowledge and intelligence of the
    silver-jacketed boy.
He is a prestidigitator. He gives coin and card and scarf
    trick shows
at picnics and advertises in his father's trade newspaper.
    He too
is embarrassed by the fat boy who cannot speak for
    himself and the
fat boy's mother, who herself makes her son sound so
    incompetent and

foolish. I want to carry off the silver-jacketed boy for a
    lover,
and to tell the fat one to murder his fat mother.

(At this point, a new show commences on stage.)

The magician dances
on stage
with thin shiny shoes,
and fast talk, making us laugh.
He introduces his trick, which will utilize a deck of
    cards,
in a convincing, firm spiel,
and in holding up the deck, reveals
that he has shaking hands.

Oh, how·can a prestidigitator have shaky hands?
But he does, and my own heart starts beating faster,
remembering my own shaky hands,
my failures as a pianist. But his shaking hands make no
    mistakes,
changing the cards from box to box until
we are all astonished,
and have no further fear for his sureness.

Then, he summons a young girl from the audience,
just as I, at my 6th grade Halloween carnival, was called
    out
of the audience.
And from his breast pocket, his trembling hand extracts
a tiny pistol, perhaps three inches long,
about which he jokes and which he insists will be
    harmless
though shootable.

When he finally gets the girl to fire it,
she jumps with fright. But it is only a cap pistol,
and we all laugh with relief at its loud discharge.

Now, he tells her, she will shoot a hole through the card
    she selects
and buries again in the deck. How this will happen
we don't know. But she aims, shoots, and seemingly
nothing happens,
till he rifles through the pack,
and finds her card—how did he know it was hers? WE
had seen it;
not he.

And sure enough,
there it is:
a tiny bullet hole in the card,
one which had not been there when she first selected it
from the deck.

I cannot explain why this afternoon with The Boy
    Magicians
or any time I spend with
illusionists, prestidigitators, or any magician
means so much to me. The
answer lies
somewhere in my unlived life, I think.
A world in which my bureau drawers contain a hundred
    colored
scarves, a room full of doves, and sitting on the closet
    shelf,
a black top hat, under which a rabbit
sometimes moves.

   * * *

Robert Kelly,
magician of the flesh, always having
known of the possible
transformations,
you are not in charge of the following episode, but you
dominate it with
                    the diabolical
power
of will
you know
            beyond
Olson,
beyond
Creeley, beyond any
of the masters.
What does this make you?
Master of Masters? Or Chief
magician,
priest,
autonomous namer?

To a garage at Bard College,
Matt Phillips has brought us; we
are jumbled from the encounter of flesh,
and all voices are ringing
with the possibility of vision.
The doves ripple their throaty voices
like plucked instruments,
warble even within
the covered cages.
Why are they white? The doves which
appear and disappear?
                    Oh, black.
Oh, white,

strumming on the old banjo,
                    Fee, Fi,
Fidlie, I, Oh,
Strumming on the Old Banjo.
Matt, who paints exquisite small
watercolors,
wears his black evening clothes
and top hat
in this country garage
on a Saturday morning,
the scarves appearing and disappearing in his hands
like fish darting among rocks and sea anemones.
Oh, where will the doves go?
Oh, where has Kelly's flesh gone?
Into the dream book?
Into the banjo?
Into his hands?
                    How did I float on that platform
in my pirate costume?
Age 11,
without wires or support of any
kind?
How did illusion shape my
life?

* * *

Houdini

she loved him.
And he could pick any lock,
first with his hands,
then learning to use his toes,
finally hands themselves tied and shoes on feet,
using the teeth.

The Teeth
which form words
against tongue and
lips.
What is language but
the motion of tongue pressed against palate
tooth
lip?

The knots of speech.
Bound to speech
as if words were knots.
But the gift
                floating
                levitation.
He passes the hoops around my body to show
there are no wires or strings.
                        The body floating
as it only could
by magic.

* * *

Houdini, give me
toe and tooth language.
Oh, hissing Pythoness of Delphi!
Oh, Kelly of the Flesh Dream Book!
Oh, pirate, bookworm, fisherman, little girl-self
who still loves Boy Magicians,
give me the ultimate magic,
that gift Creeley offers,
the word,
one word,
not "magic"

LISTEN,
             the word changes as it hisses
             out of the wet ground
             in Matt Phillips' garage,

"truth"
      but that can't be,
      now I hear
"beauty"
          now
"truth" again.

But my ears deceive me,
just as my eyes allow the deception of
Illusionists.

I leave you with this image, floating,
      a shiny bumblebee pirate,
      ascending a stage,
      glowing like a firefly,
      this child floating on the stage
      with the aid of Black Silk Tophat
      floating
      floating
      in a pool of silver,
      out of the fire of daylight,
      into the glint of black and silver night,
      floating,
      in birth,
      floating,
      as an ancient fish,
      scaly, glistening, the cold lips
      waiting for a word

                              Silver
                              Truth
                              Fish
                              Beauty
                              Night
and finally to know
that it is not the precise word itself

but
articulation.
Articulation we demand. The bullet hole, tiny & precise,
        in the
mystery card.

Darwin's magic.

Freedom from savagery.

Un Morceau en Forme de Poire

for Thomas Parkinson

Sitting on my kitchen table
in its yellow enamelled cast iron pot
is the remains of a liquid for poaching pears
which contains caterpillars of lemon peel
and centipede lengths of vanilla bean.
The morning kitchen has a country smell,
for my sink is stopped up,
and I couldn't wash the dishes last night
after working on my Hazelnut Chocolate Pear Torte,
and the thick porcelain jacketed top of my bain-marie
        has smudges
like muddy prints
over its lip, waiting for sudsy hot water and a drain
that will work.

The fragrances of vanilla and chocolate and pear mingle
with some beets and onions, waiting on the counter
for soup.
Reminding me of a moment
in my life
which perhaps was a bridge between
the girl who ate ham sandwiches on white bread with
        mayonnaise & a pickle
on Saturday evenings,
as an after-library-and-shopping treat,
and the woman who now makes Sacher Tortes,
linguine al pesto,
or stuffed vine leaves
commonly on Saturday nights.

This scene from the '50s:
        wearing the cap of darkness,
        I go to babysit for some young university faculty.
        Entering their house in the Berkeley hills, I see
        plain pine floors with
        threadbare Oriental carpets,
        bookshelves made of boards and bricks,
        hand thrown pottery.
        They leave, and I hold the baby
        as he cries himself to sleep.
        Then I wander about the small house into the
            kitchen
        where every dish, glass, pot or pan
        seems to be dirty on the sink,
        the kitchen table holding Chemex coffee pot with
            a bit of
        amber liquid
        in the bottom,
        next to it, on a saucer, a paper filter full of wet
            grounds.
        The whole kitchen was permeated
        with the smell of vanilla biscuits,
        and a mingle of other interesting possibilities.
            Some
        leeks? The Viennese Roast coffee beans? Some
            rusks
        which were also lying out?
For the first time in my life
I witnessed a soiled kitchen, used by sloppy people,
which seemed wholesome, the dirt and insects of
        gardens, rather than
neglect;
fragrant
with good food and even
a good life. Of course I spent

the evening washing the dishes
and cleaning the kitchen,
embarrassing the good-livers when they came home,
who felt required to offer me
more money.
                I, too,
was embarrassed,
for what I really
wanted
was to belong to the world they did,
where mess and chaos had the smell
of vanilla.
                What a difference
between my mother's sense of good food
(baked ham and canned peas)
and this kitchen,
redolent with rosemary, lamb shoulder and garlic,
an odor I didn't know then, because I thought garlic was
        a stale
white powder with a slightly bitter taste.

That moment
going into the kitchen
gave me a new possibility for
ORDER.
Am I destined
I wonder
to go back to the Berkeley hills someday
and live in such a house,
the messy interesting life of those young intellectuals?
        My own
kitchen here in the midwest has acquired
some of its jumble.

Perhaps last night

across the continent
that couple, now undoubtedly in their 60s
woke up
to a distant fragrance
of poaching pears,
a torte baking,
the ganache cream being stirred with its 15 ounces of
    chocolate?

Perhaps, in a dream, they saw me
as an old woman of the earth,
holding their son by the heel,
immersing him in the fire of my passionate need
trying to forge the armor of immortality
as he cried himself to sleep,
after which I went into the kitchen
and ritually cleansed it,
leaving some clarity, leaving it renewed,
and taking with me the knowledge
of common chaos,
mortal beauty,
smelling of vanilla,
an earthy bean.

WINTER

Molokai

for Travis Summersgill

This is the island
where a best friend became an alcoholic
putting vodka and orange juice in his thermos
each morning, after
sleeping all night in his clothes,
and going to Molokai High each day drunk,
to teach *The Old Man and the Sea.*

Here,
an eight-year-old boy shot another eight-year-old
with his father's pistol
after being taunted for hanging out his
mother's washing.

Here, native teenagers rape tourists
who camp alone
on deserted beaches and
acquire reputations for *machismo* with
their similar friends. These same
teenagers
whose accomplishments also include murder
sit in another friend's high school classroom
and give her a hard time
because she is beautiful and "talks funny."
They are known in the school to the authorities as
"The Rapists,"
and will remain in school for more than a year,
unreprimanded,
before ever
coming up before the juvenile authorities.

This is the island
where I fall asleep smelling the fragrance
of Norman's gardenias.

Here we live in an apartment overlooking the ocean.
Our downstairs neighbors
proudly
possess a light which hangs
purple and fluorescent on the porch
each night,
                electrocuting bugs.
Every bug hisses,
snaps,
pops,
as if it were part of a big mess of barbequing spareribs.
Occasionally a long crackle is heard. We think
that sound must mean
a gecko
has lost its pale life.
All night
the smell of the gardenias by my bed
and the sound of frying insects
downstairs.

This is the island where Baker lives on a houseboat
and schemes about paddle-wheels walking over coral
        reefs.
If I told you Baker drove a jeep,
you would get the wrong picture/ it is
the four wheels and chassis-bed
of a Volkswagen,
a motor sitting in the front,
like a cake of ice in a wooden box,
roll bars, front and back, which look like
the old metal frames of a bed,

seats made of old dinette chairs,
their chrome legs removed.
And he's painted it like a leopard
I suppose
because he drives it on this jungle island of Molokai
and parks it in a palm grove where
there is
a sign saying
BEWARE OF FALLING COCONUTS.
He parks it there because he lives on a houseboat
in the shallow water before the coral reef,
a bachelor
who lives surrounded by ocean and with no running
    water.
We talk a lot about Baker,
but seldom to him.
Perhaps because he's a raconteur and his life is filled
    with better
stories
than any of us could ever devise. Perhaps Baker's life
is a mythic life of adventure,
because he does exist
surviving from day to day,
like a continuous mountain climber,
deep-sea diver,
spelunker,
sky diver,
aerialist.

Baker reminisces about his past/
all his lives—
as a Navy seal,
as a grizzly bear hunter in Washington State parks,
as a logger, builder,
entrepreneur—

and says that some of his best days
were
when he and one of his wives
lived with orange crates for furniture
and whenever they had to move,
they just packed up their belongings
into the orange crates,
put them into the truck and moved on.

Baker's mother,
part Indian,
a woman who's lived on the fringe of poverty and
      ignominy all her
Western life,
came to visit him on his houseboat after we left Molokai.
Our friends tell us that she is a wizened old lady,
wearing black chinos, chain-smoking Lucky Strikes,
who neatly deposits her cigarette ash
in her trouser cuffs
rather than use an ash tray.

This is the island where Baker
drives his leopard-spotted jeep,
barrelling up and down the roads with his old mother,
both of them having a beer.
Here, there is not one single stoplight
and, like Alaska,
the roads often simply end in a forest.

Here is where a shattered Vietnam veteran
whose child was lost but magically unharmed in the rain
      forest
lives.

And here is where a burnt-out guitarist lives because
drugs are easy to come by.

Here, the Baha'i faith prospers,
and there are extraordinary numbers of other small
    churches.

Here, is the most famous leper colony
in the world
which has now become a tourist attraction.

Molokai,
I hear in your name, the word
MOLOCH,
the terrible Canaanite god-King to whom children were
    burnt in sacrifice
and remember smelling at night
the kiawe wood burning in kilns as it was transformed
    into charcoal.
I imagine
inside those kilns
the glowing fires that reiterate
the island's volcanic past.

When I lived there
I lived close to the center of life,
molten burning center of
destruction.

Making a Sacher Torte

Her hands, like albino frogs,
on the keys of a Bosendorfer,
nails short and thin like sliced almonds, fleshy fingers,
with the lightning bolt gold and diamond wedding
ring, zigzagging up to her fat knuckle,
looking out of place
on the heavy working hand.

Forty-five and fashionable,
with knit suits and suede pumps on thin-ankled feet,
short, curly blond hair and her big Jewish nose,
her husband a jeweler and she, with her rich German
        accent,
my piano tutor.

I, 19, and wearing home-made cotton dresses with
        gathered skirts,
the Niagara Falls in my eyes, no wedding, no wedding,
a girl with nothing but soapy hands and wet heart, a big
        frog-like brain;
I loved her for listening to me.
On the black piano bench, I was still the little princess
        whose golden
ball
had rolled into a well, and she,
the Frog Prince, lifted it out
with webbed hands, tossing it in the light, the gold
of her lightning bolt wedding ring catching the sun, as
        she gave me
her gold, the talk, the princess world of pianos;
        converting me

from Chopin who had a perfect hand, like a water lily,
to Beethoven's last work, fashioned with shovels and
    clubs
and the Germanic ear for long phrases, never-ending
    sentences, who
too must have had hands that looked more like
pads than the lily.

Near Christmas, she asked me one afternoon,
"Do you know what I have spent the last two days doing
    with these hands?"
(spreading them out,
heavy and short-nailed against the piano keys)
"Grinding nuts in a mortar. For a torte." And she
    continued to talk
about her culinary activities which seemed exotic then
    to me
and which I only recalled today after I had whirled some
    almonds
in my Cuisinart and was folding them into meringue for
    a Sacher Torte,
living a life so remote from those sad Berkeley days
when I was a poor student, poor adolescent, girl from the
    working classes
where the piano bench, hard seat, was the only one I
    wanted;
on which I sat five hours most days,
beating my hands on the keys, out of love, as she had
    ground those nuts
by hand for her family's holiday cake.

* * *

We often talked of our favorite books and both of us were
    then avidly
reading Salinger's stories as they were published in *The
    New Yorker.*
I, wishing the Glass family was my own and she,
    preaching, of all
things, about how I should have more charitable feelings
    for my mother.
Yet, my own mother had none of the attributes which
    made Mrs. Ury
so compelling to me; for it was not just those hours at
    the piano
that made me cherish her. She was a bold and intelligent
    woman who
had forced her family to understand their danger in
    Germany and arranged
for them to leave before the disaster of the camps. She
    lived in a
world of books and pianos, had gone on tour all over the
    world,
could make her Linzer Torte without any machine. She
    spoke two
languages flawlessly and was generous of spirit, though a
    perfection-
ist of craft, to this provincial girl who couldn't play the
    piano very
well. She talked to me by the hour, wearing elegant
    clothes, and
praised me when I deserved it. Once, I remember her
    telling me about
practicing the piano in winter in Germany, when she
    was a student,
and wearing wool gloves with the finger-ends cut off,
    because it was

so cold in the studio. She gave me a sense of the meaning
    of sacri-
fice, and in retrospect
what I feel my own family most deprived me of was
that meaning.
That if you practiced the piano in a studio at 45 degrees
    in winter
it was in order to become an exceptional performer
of the world's great piano music.
That those same hands
wearing a $10,000 ring,
30 years later,
could perform the same kind of act,
as a ritual for her family,
grinding the nuts for the Christmas torte,
when, of course, her maid could
have done it
just as well.

And for me, a new meaning for the Frog Prince:
Not the lover, whose kindness made him beautiful.
That seems like a small meaning for the fairy tale.
Rather, that the transformation itself
of Frog into Prince can happen. That Mrs. Ury,
with her great frog hands, who could play with the verve
    of Rubinstein
and the delicacy of Gieseking, rescued the ball of gold
after it rolled into the well,
gave me her German self as mother,
gave me a new history, gave me
herself in marriage; for though I have not become a
    concert pianist,
I have accepted the tradition of the keyboard artists.
And her great gift to me:
to show me that impossible as it was for me to be a
    musician

in fact
this did not deprive me of music, but gave it back to me
	in more complex ways.

As the torte was baking in the oven, today,
I wondered idly about
how different my life would have been had Tanya Ury
	actually
been my mother. But of course the truth
is that she was;
how accidental is blood; how meaningless
the connection of birth. I look in the pond,
a mirror full of lilies whose long root systems curl up
	from the
chocolatey mud and whose green leaves might hold one
	of those
green music makers. In it
I see nothing but a reflection of sunlight, a golden spot
which must be projected through the thick lenses of my
	glasses.
As I move my face, the golden
spot dances and rolls over the water,
over the lily pads, occasionally
reflecting and glinting off one of the pale pink flower
	buds;
experience and memory are my real roots,
tangled, complicated, all the freeways I have traveled
to reach this moment when I lift the firm almond torte
out of the oven.

Little Tricks of Linear B

The beginning was the dream,
and the voice was a turban gourd.
A strum.
What are we hiding?
Our new bodies
born underground with pearls of old corn?
Our dry husks
on the winter-hard ground/ Where
is the moment
between wet rotting
and ashy desiccation? The beginning was
a dream.
But what country is shaped
like an ear of corn?
Which one like a bunch of grapes?
Which one, a pomegranate?
What map leads to the chrysalis nut?

THE DREAM

I was afraid to move my head or neck. I
realized that stiff branches of little black
grapes, like nubbins of Concords, only jet
black, were protruding out of my head. My
face also was covered with black nodules, but
these were velvety clusters, like grapes but
spread flat over the lower face, not protruding
like the head grapes. The feeling I had was of
horror at the moistness and simultaneous
stiffness of the new grape spikes on my head,

and I knew that if I tried to touch them they might pop and squirt a bloody juice. Helplessly, I knew they were a vegetation disease coming out of my body, like a beautiful but malevolent fungus, and that I must do something at once. The only solution that seemed possible was to break large 1,000 unit capsules of golden oily Vitamin E, all over my scalp. I felt the viscous honey-colored oil cover and seep into my head and felt that if anything could heal me, it would be the Vitamin E. But I knew it would have to remain covering the erect little grape-bunch knobs for a long time before it could dissolve them. And that I would be sticky, messy and uncomfortable as well as untouchable for some time. Still, I felt hopeful as I woke up, that the Vitamin E would heal this vegetable disease. When I awoke I felt bathed in the Vitamin E oil, as if in a warm sunshine.

What country is shaped like an ear of corn?
    California.
    The Golden State.
    From which I fled, but now dream of. Does
    it matter where anyone belongs?
    Do we have a choice? Grinding the corn for
        tortillas
    I think of myself as smokey flesh
    hung to dry in the midwest. Jerky,
    smoked meat. Yet, it is not California I long for.
    But my youth.
    Not golden but moist. The spiky grapes of my
        young tongue,
    the moistness of my mushroom body.

In a cheap roadside restaurant this week
I saw a poor family, traveling
for the holidays.

> At the table was a fat man with scuffed shoes
> and greasy hair, a squashed spongy nose and
> bad teeth: the father. The mother: his small,
> mean-faced wife. With them was another man
> who had grease-stained hands and skinny
> body, and wore a beard which protruded from
> his face bushily, as if it were about to fly away.
> There were several children with frog-like
> faces, including a fat teenage girl with the
> father's bulbous squashy nose spread across
> her face. She was the one who interested me.
> Though I found them all repulsive—I was also
> fascinated. The girl was a graceless person but
> obviously newly aware of her sex and flirting
> with the man with the brush beard. As I
> looked at her I realized that her youth, the
> freshness of her ugly (not even very clean or
> well-groomed) face and body was undeniable
> to anyone over forty. At first I thought, how
> pathetic. To have only youth and nothing
> else. But then I realized that *I* had never had
> more than that. This girl was myself as I had
> refused to see myself. In the past. Even now. I
> moved my hand to my head and touched my
> scalp to see if the spiky grapes were still there.

She lives in a country shaped like
an ear of corn; no,
this one is a pomegranate, the seeds still fresh and
bloody, and stiff as corn, thick with juice,
as the nubby bunches of grapes growing out of my head
had been.

49

Oh, little girl. Oh,
Marsh King's daughter,
why are you here,
in my life today?

THE MARSH KING'S DAUGHTER

Her feet,
stuck in a loaf of pumpernickel bread, as pun-
ishment/ for her bad behaviour—
    pulling off the wings of flies,
    tormenting the cat,
    not obeying her parents—
she is banished to the mud and algae of the
    marsh,
immovable in her loaf,
to be crawled over by insects,
hissed at by snakes,
with toads and frogs hopping in her hair.
This is the punishment:
to remain in the Marsh Kingdom
until someone whom she has mistreated
voluntarily
comes to rescue her. Oh,
little girl. I know now
why you are here
and not in the land shaped like an ear of corn,
not even in the pomegranate map,
or under the grape arbor.
The heavy loaf holds you in this swampy place,
weighed down by grain,
stuck in dough.

I am a faun, a satyr, my head
is horned with knobby stiff grape bunches.
The black is obsidian, polished,
but the black rot is mold on my face.
I am grinning
but in pain. Lechery
does not interest me,
but my form is set, appearance
false to myself. The grapes,
my horns,
the horns I should not have.

Who will rescue the Marsh King's daughter?
Not the ant with missing legs.
Nor the grasshopper with cracked thorax.
Not the blind toad.
Not mother who kneaded her into the loaf
and stuck her feet-first into the oven.
Not father who is away
sailing the Pacific.
Not brother who helped her set butterflies
on fire in glass jars.
Nor anyone from the country shaped like
an ear of corn,
for that voice
is distant, distant

THE DREAM RELATED TO ANOTHER DREAM

In this dream, a terrifying figure, white with black spots,
the head of a borzoi with sharp teeth and the appearance
of a jester, stands in the hall outside my room. I am not

sure if it is myself standing there, inside this figure, but whether it is a monster or myself, I am frightened of it. The black spots are intense and a source of evil. I know I am in danger. This figure is somehow the same as myself in the vegetation dream. The grapes had the same intensity as these black spots on the white jester.

THE DREAM AGAIN

Is focused on my head. I really do not see
my body at all. Only my head.

The predominant sensation is one of
new growth. The stiff bunches of little
black grapes are just emerged from my head,
and are vulnerable beneath their tense skin.
Easy to crush. My fear is that they will
break and bleed and spread the disease as
well as disfiguring me, for I am certain
that they are a cancerous growth
which will destroy me. My face too is covered with the growth, but here it takes the
flat fuzzy form of black felt or velvet. Like
a web, it spreads over my face from
near the mouth. I keep wanting to
touch my face and head but am afraid I will
disturb the growth. I begin to break the cylin-
drical Vitamin E capsules over my head.
The warm golden oil runs in
rivulets to my brow and finally
down onto my cheeks. I know it is healing
my growths and can erase them.

What does the Marsh King's daughter think
while she is plummeting headfirst
into the swamp?
She, baked in the loaf,
which will weigh her down
always
in the swamp.
Does she repent her life
or only think with anger of the mother who
baked her into the loaf,
of the wandering father,
of the painful world which she wanted to destroy?
And now another pain: the swamp itself,
the Marsh King,
her new father,
whom she will never see.

FINAL DREAM NARRATION

Wanting to touch the sprigs of grapes but
afraid they will burst. Feeling them growing
out of my tight scalp, I know they are
diseased and are nearly full grown. Wanting to put my fingers on the juicy knobs but
knowing I will make matters worse if I touch
them. I break the Vitamin E capsules like
honey over my head. Maybe this will cure, or
at least prolong my life? The growths on my
face do not concern me as do the horns of
grapes emerging from my head. It is them I
must heal.

The Marsh King
rules the state shaped like
an ear of corn. But I
rule the pomegranate
map.
Yet, it is in the state of the grape
where the Marsh King's daughter has been thrown
into her father's swamp, her feet baked
into her mother's heavy bread.
These three countries will be a scene
of desolation, and the
landscape
for healing.
              First the Vitamin E
will bathe and soothe the woman with grapes
growing out of her scalp.
Then she will break the bread
from the soft white feet
of the Marsh King's daughter.
Then, oh, then, she
will offer a glass of wine to the Marsh King.
She will perform all these rituals in the land
shaped like an ear of corn.

But what if the Sunshine oil does not cancel the growth?
Black, rotting, fertile with death.
What if the loaf has ossified and the soft white feet
of the Marsh King's daughter must be
sliced off with the loaf?
What if the wine is refused
by the Marsh King who is a beer drinking football player,
and what if the state shaped like an ear of corn
is nibbled away by mice?
What if the Hollywood itself is transformed into a heron
      and flies away?

Where will George Washington,
looking for hot countries, be?
Will the King of Spain ever acknowledge
the Marsh King or
his footless daughter?

What if dream does not inform us but, instead,
rules the world?
The Marsh King's daughter
with her bleeding legs, footless,
cannot even walk home
after she has been dragged out of the swamp.
Will my grape horns turn to rock?
Will the chrysalis nut ever be cracked, only to reveal
a stone butterfly inside?
Not,
will the story be told,
but
what *is* the story?

Who speaks the truth?

Sally Plum

*for Sally Arteseros, who has never
liked her name*

velvet,
soft as a mouse,
but the color of Satsuma;
mauve silk & seed pearls;
you said you
hate your name
but don't really know of one that suits you.

Tonight I serve
Plum Pudding, soaked in cognac for a month,
its currants plump with boozy waiting.
The hard sauce is as smooth as an egg.
The bombe
in its amber pool of Rémy Martin,
burning,
sustains a cloud
like blue bachelor buttons
or swamp gas,
will-o'-the-wisp caught on a plate.
I think of autumn bonfires
in a world of pumpkins, wheat and sheep.
The wanderer camping
in his van,
a lonely figure walking over a moor,
on a crackling night.

In a drawing room somewhere
with another name,
perhaps Elizabeth or Charlotte or Mirabelle,

you would be wearing your new plum coloured velvet
with a bonnet to match,
and then you would dream of another time
when there would be more to do than
reading
or singing Schumann.
And you would wish your name less staid,
more friendly,
a name like Sally
which might allow you to travel unchaperoned with a
      man
in a railway carriage, or
would you long
for another culture?

black hair?

rice-white face?

and a name like Satsuma/
                    Sally Plum?

The Ice Queen's Calla Lily Fingers

Little girl, whose socks were always lost
in the scuffed heels
of her shoes,
your face like a round moon showing curdy
like a blemish
in the daylight sky, the world says
you got things wrong.

Did the hibiscus of Southern California,
the humming birds like plums,
the hot air
distort your life?

You saw the Snow Queen
riding in her crystal sleigh,
not
as evil
but as refreshing goodness.
Her sky, a mirror of ice,
and its cracking splinters
NOT giving a false view of the world
but transforming
squalid or mundane reality into
an acceptable world.
                    Where did
the slivers of ice
stuck in my own eye
come from
in this land of orange trees
and sweet dates?

Now winter is the major season
in my life. And I contradict
the world that ice
is evil
or a signal of doom.
I know, I was not wrong,
seeing through the glassy fragment in my eye
winter's truth.
The Ice Queen
robed in ermine draws up to my door,
her crystal sleigh
invisible; her calla lily fingers
touch my door.
I go to greet her,
past tears,
wearing a cap of darkness,
the world frozen
against pain.

Paleolithic

Once the desert sucked poison
out of my body.
The sun
drawing the juices of anger
from my fibers.
I gladly went to poolside,
sat on hot beaches,
lived in sultry climates,
was never photographed not wearing dark glasses for the
    glare.

Now my body is oyster white,
soft and innocent,
sucked clean.
How can I survive in this world?
The sun burns me now.
The air contaminates me.
In heat I perish.
Those poisons were my hostage.
Now,
sucked clean
I'm innocent.

And dying.

Jekyl Island

The plantation oaks, like abstract sculptures,
give the island its shape.
We have come here
to look at the ocean,
walk on the beach,
see the shapes and gestures of the trees,
search for good things to eat,
and we do those things as the tourists we are,
and you watch television
while I sit in scenic spots around the hotel
reading my books.

For us, going to a new place
means doing those same few things we do everywhere,
me, reading and writing,
you, photographing and looking.
The rain pours down for a whole day,
wind whips the surf to almost frozen sugary peaks
and people here for a golf vacation
and those who came for boating or fishing
are clustered in miserable huddles.
Some days I envy them,
swimming in bright pools,
walking miles with their clubs,
constantly checking out gear,
but today I realize
that our way
has much to be said for it.
I need only a nook to retire to,
my big book bag always stuffed with everything I need,
and you with an eye

which enjoys recording anything
        rain
        sun
        sleet.
Now the water drips from the live oaks
and a brilliant sun comes out of
the cloudy sky.
Perhaps this radiance will only last
half an hour before another squall
blows in.
But we will walk out through the jungle of plants
to the boardwalk
and down to the beach.
Bad weather or good,
our day is the same.

I do
bless
my sedentary habits.

L'Enfant Terrible

A single letter
kills my grandfather.
                    "A"
You are dead.
            "B"
We'll bury you.
                "C"
                        No, stop. The letters
make it all seem terrible. I died
fifty years ago. Let me remain
your dead relative.

These words
made up of letters
                    "N"
"O"
    Sometimes
                "I" then
"d"   "o"   "n"   "t"   "l"   "o"   "v"   "e"   "y"
        "o"   "u"

How does this old corpse know?
He listened to the singing?
A tree.
I found this under a tree.
Just one touch of the moist claveria,
lace against wood.
The letters of the alphabet are deadly
to those who cannot/
                    read.

Human History: Its Documents

Sometimes poison
a decoration
in our lives/ or more.
                    Black oily
French Roast
coffee beans, ground and
brewed,
steaming in a cup/ the day still with no wasted and
      empty
words
in it,
          thick cream
floating on the beverage,
the memory of a silver pot and a silk coverlet
somewhere behind
this desirable poison,

hot from the oven
flaky butter dough, a beautiful parchment
croissant,
the fingers covered with a film
of grease,
the flour milled empty of
nurture,
appeasing the eye and tongue, like
delicate crumpled stiff letters
in the belly,
the cream which would bloat the stomachs of
African children/ we have evolved too far
to digest it;
these poisons ARE TREATS

to start special mornings, as if
I were the woman in
her peignoir
on Sunday Morning,
listening for the beat of giant bird wings,
pterodactyl,
the big poetic line
I wait for,
with these poisons I long for.

Spring coming and I fantasize Hot Cross Buns,
all of civilization summed up
in dough,
bean,
viney resins,
and the paper, the ink
which allows us to transmit
our recipes.
I, standing in line to do my monthly banking
watch a young pregnant mother lean over to her
        two-year-old
and stuff into his unwilling mouth
a piece of candy. She is grinning and nodding, as if she
        were in a
Punch and Judy show. "Good," she is saying, as the child
        grimaces and
drools and finally chews his little pellet of poison sugar.
        She
beams
to us all,
as we stand in line with checks and bills. How good she
        believes
herself to be, having just begun one young child's craving
for poison. Food
that will never nourish

and, in this case, didn't even
please.

Yes, how I hated that school teacher's phrase, "You can
    trap more flies
with honey than with vinegar." As if we were all going
    out there
to read *Song of Myself* and *Howl*
to a large swarm of irritating flies.

Wrenching Grace

these paradoxes
which govern daily life
                    and how
much
        do   we all deserve?

Why am I still angry at a man who scathed me
18 years ago in *Kulture*?

My stomach ache this morning/
from 18 years ago?

Is grace
abstinence?

Or perhaps   more possible   in empty times
purity/ denial.

Empty words.

The value: their emptiness?

The Dark Procession

*to the man who rides for the Pony
Express*

I go to the West
to look for you. This aloe plant
whose fleshy fingers I break off
rubbing their clear jelly
on my rough hands
is that West.
The tequila in its glass bottle
as clear as the aloe's inner moisture
and the hard-skinned wet lime
which is added to the tequila
—they are the West.
The hibiscus yellow cushions
on my sofa and chairs
where I sit
are the West,
even though the sun which streams into this apartment
is not the West.
                    The Beethoven
I listen to on the stereo
is not Vienna;
it is California,
and my stumbling days as a young
awkward student
where only at the piano I possessed some grace.
I long for the West
and the perfect receipt of letters.
Sitting here I listen for hoof beats, clattering up
the driveway.
Perhaps men

who love other men
still write letters to women,
though they do not come into the dark-balconied
night
        when we long for them.
So I wait for the Pony Express.
How can a woman live
when she has only a root of men who love other men
in her past?
Her father who lived as a sailor on board ships
preferring card games, boiler rooms and aircraft carriers
to a kitchen and bedrooms with three women;
the lonely high school organist
who at fifteen was already haunting the gay bars of
        Corona del Mar,
Laguna, Long Beach;
the midwestern grad student
who was so kind and took her to poetry readings and
        never touched
her, though she didn't know why;
the dark English professor of poetry who rode
        motorcycles,
wore leather and was also so untouchingly kind;
then you, from the Pony Express,
the rider who galloped into New York and teased your
        lover with me
making him believe you might actually
opt for a woman;
Sheriff Day who came along glittering and seductive,
a silver star pinned over his crotch,
knowing this girl from the West loved disguises and
        taboos
and could be taken for a long ride,
who burned up her first novel in his fireplace, a final act
of bitchiness, and the beginning

of her long despair;
oh, the list is too long and could go on
for pages. What can I expect
or any other woman whose father was Walt Whitman,
a man who gently loved all men
as mankind
as the young soldier who creates
a nation?
So,
I long for the West
even though it has never given me
a lover,
only cowboys who stick to their horses,
that sheriff,
and you, the Rider from the Pony Express,
bringing me letters, letters,
letters I finally cannot answer,
because they are never, never
from a father,
       brother,
       a lover or husband,
those men are
and always will be
in the company of other men,
drinking,
watching football games,
playing cards,
and if they are writing,
it is not letters to me,
but to other men,
love letters even,
or documents of state.

The Dark Procession, Reviewed

My body glistens,
snail moon,
delicate lettuce leaf breasts,
cucumber skin,
pale moistness of early summer/ and
the fantasy boys I long for,
        blond surfers and skiers,
        black scorpion musicians,
        Whitmanian sculptors,
enter as solstice images:
the dream-code
marks each one.
        ("Ms. Wakoski," says my seal-sleek
        bright student, wearing corn-golden
        t-shirt and skirt over her Easter tan, the
        gold chains coiling on neck and fingers,
        "is Galway Kinnell still alive?" She is
        preparing her oral book review. "He was
        born in 1927. That would make him
        pretty old, if he's still alive." Only ten
        years older than me, I think. "Yes, he's
        alive. He would only be about 54," I say,
        firmly. Wondering if anyone
        understands that the longing of youth
        does not pass away with middle age.
        Not even with old age.)
Tonight, the full moon sits outside my window
a beach ball
and shines its light on the shadow of
my girl-body.
The moon shines on seeds of Jerusalem Cherry,

rooting into a ball of fronds for me in new soil,
and on the football shaped magnolia buds,
thrusting their scaly pistols into Georgia night,
and into my longing brain, spinning
which has been set in patterns of love,
for years,
cannot resist one more
fantasy.
I sleep long long hours
under this moon,
for the procession of lovers, always
best in imagination, is long
and while the real life is dark with pain,
with outlaws, cowboys, the military, and lovers
of men, there is another life,
of novas, young
exploding men
of light
who love me with Apollonian grace,
who worship me through poems and
letters
let the loving remain perfect
because never fulfilled.
Tonight I dream of Craig,
           who rescued my Jerusalem Cherry (with mealy
               bugs) from the
           wastebasket,
           and who haunted my office this winter, foraging
               for sugar,
           and who had just asked me to judge a poetry
               contest between him
           and Paul Murphy for the prize of a pound of
               M & Ms,
           with his soft voice and unreadable handwriting,

          his slanting eyes and golden self in love with
               John Lennon, as
I have in the past,
dreamed, luxuriously, of
          Steve, the California runner from my high school
               town,
          with football shoulders and the wonderful poem
               about eating
          Christmas dinner at McDonalds,
          who stood on my doorstep in grey
          running clothes reminding me that I dared not
               touch
          any one I really loved,
or Gary, another big blond man with high cheekbones,
     soft voice and
          a hidden self that blossomed only within secret
               relationships,
or Jim, of another time, who was studying to be an
     architect and loved
          the football coach's daughter, and who with his tall
               golden
          body offered only the secret love of never touching
          a final sexual impulse, the impulse that creates
               longing and
          can never annul it,
or Robert, whom I longed for in Majorca, while he drank
     and ignored me
          except for the lonely unnoticed conversations we
               had
          in the lane by the bake shop or on the path near the
               torrente.
Is this the real procession
in my life?

Not dark, but hidden?
The men who allowed me
sensuousness, completely
fulfilled by the longing itself?
Would I rather fantasize
than touch?

The moon stirs this body tonight.
Pale lettuce, gone to seed,
grown tall and feathery,
a ruffled pagoda, a false shape,
the delicate leaves
we desire to make up our salad.
the moonlit lettuce patch,
pale leaves,
pale leaves, under the snail moon.
Reflected light,
from the golden lover hidden behind sea-grey eyes?

SPRING

Frog Mozart

Rain
transforming our apartment parking lot
into a pond
        and in late spring
it is filled with frogs
who lift their voices like a new kind of rain,
breathing in and out,
drop-like notes, spattering them across the parking lot
into my cave-room
where I sit reading in a warm pool of light.
                Like a giant chandelier
                moving in a breeze,
                the sound sways and tinkles.
Summer has dried up most of this
civil pond. Only a
basin the size of two Volkswagens is left. The cattails
which grow
at the edge
are drying out, with ragged fur on their
brushes.
At dusk, I come out on my balcony
after a steaming day,
stand among my potted plants
and see
in the parking lot pool
a killdeer
hopping,
bathing in the pond. His clear
tooting voice
utters one or two notes
as he jumps in and out of the water,

grooming for his evening.
I remember that what I love
is the managed world,
the juxtaposition of mowed lawn and
small untouched copse of wood,
of marsh and
parking lot,
of all my passions
but still
       sleeping in a trim bed
with smooth cotton sheets,
perhaps printed with a green and orange and white jungle
    of flowers,
many goose feather pillows in neat cases,
and a silk cover
I can touch.
I like to see the world
from behind glass,
and to stay in away from the mosquitoes.
As beautiful as the voices of the frogs
were
on late spring nights,
they could not replace Beethoven,
Mozart,
Ravel, Debussy. Yet the continuity
and the concatenation—
      an evening of Mozart,
      ended as I turn out the lights and
      open the balcony door,
      to hear the frogs, as loud as my stereo had earlier
        sounded,
      their voices plinking and
      zinging, humming and sawing, reassuring me that
      two worlds
      co-exist,

and I can
            at least
listen
to them both.

Green Thumb

How can we trace this
genetically?

There were two Pearls
in my mother's family. Both
eccentric
independent
and gardeners.
They were not related. I don't actually know
if they even
knew each other.
From two different generations.
But oddly similar. Both had warbly,
marbly voices, not deep
but grating, and full of abrasive
sound. And both
had hands and fingernails
always stained
with earth.

Auntie Pearl was a relative by marriage, of my Aunt
Ella's,
that lady who bloomed
fast
like an early rose
and fell and faded as
quickly
her young husband dead
under his motorcycle
and she, left alone with two daughters
and work in an aircraft factory during World
War II,

and her husband's brother and sister,
Uncle Noah &
Auntie Pearl.

Auntie Pearl had a big old crumbling house
which seemed jumbled with possessions,
and I
remember sitting on her screened porch
with the feel of hundreds of plants
surrounding me,
healthy but, like Auntie Pearl, ungroomed,
full of dead leaves, which she never removed, all
    climbing and
growing out of their pots,
or living in ragged beds she never
beautified,
            only allowed to have a
rampant
growth.

She was one of those adults who acted as if life were full
    of dangerous
secrets,
and had conversations in which much alluding,
rolling of eyeballs and hushed voices
        were used. I felt
around Auntie Pearl
that she saw everyone's life as
overgrown
as her plants,
the world dark, damp, hiding the
unknown in its deep green foliage,
and like Uncle Noah and Aunt Ella,
Auntie Pearl belonged to a Holy Roller Church,
and thus she did see

almost everything worldly
as a sin.

Still, I never felt she really understood
the beautiful nature of her plants,
that she had deliberately created a dark jungle place,
a crawling Garden of Eden,
a place where one might sin
just in order
            to come out of the brambles.
Pearl,—how unlike a pearl Auntie Pearl was.
Yet, she had the gift of her garden,
even though she really didn't understand
plants
at all.

Always, I was frightened of her,
as if that tangled, steaming, overgrown life
had borne her as a carnivorous plant,
as if she had jaw-like traps at the ends of her leaves,
ready to spring on an insect,
or as if she were one of the tiny sundew plants which
            grows in sub-arctic
bogs,
or a pitcher plant or cobra lily full of fluid which both
            attracts
and dissolves
the insects drawn to it.
No wonder I remember Auntie Pearl:
she must have owned Southern California's Garden of
            Eden.

The other family Pearl
was the second wife of one of my cousins.
To children,

in whatever time or place,
divorce
will always be secret, an
activity surrounded by mystery.
It is a time when adults whisper
about sex,
and enumerate its offenses,
and otherwise chunky lifeless,
unappealing adults
at once
become imbued with Gothic lives. Mr.
Rochester
who was just cranky old Uncle Noah
with food stains on his tie
takes on intrigue
when you hear about the secret Mrs. Rochester
who was crazy
and, locked up in her room, set fire to the house and
burned to death.
I think that's what I felt about Uncle Noah, who was a
junk dealer
and Auntie Pearl, proprietress of her
Garden of Eden.

Pearl,
the second Pearl,
with perky sausage curls and shiny pumps
always reminded me of Little Lulu's aunt.
And while my Aunt Eva had hated her son's first wife,
Milly,
she hated even more
divorce,
and of course detested the new woman
with whom her son might try marriage
again.

But it was Pearl's green thumb
which finally united this waitress with the family,
all farmers *manqués*,
who had left the potato fields to find
better lives
but never lost their allegiance
to dirt.
So, while my Aunt Eva painted china
and collected salt and pepper shakers
until she had
over five thousand pairs,
she also subscribed to *The Farm Journal*,
and daughter-in-law Pearl gardened,
gardened,
grew her prize winning African violets
and achieved a place in the family.

Though Auntie Pearl is remembered by me for not
    having a husband,
and Pearl because she married my cousin,
I think of both of them
as women alone,
and remembering my mother—
    who loved to hint at the failure of others,
    as if hinting rather than telling proved her
        graciousness and goodwill,
      whereas it only
    made her seem
    sly and more petty—
hinting that Pearl's husband had become an alcoholic
    after he retired.
Her phrase was that he
                "Liked to bend his elbow"
too well, and she
hinted that he left home each morning

and went to the Benevolent and Protective Order of Elks
    where he drank
all day,
just to get away from Pearl's African violets
and the garden club work
which filled her life.

I don't know:
plants seem like the best kind of companions
to me, rewarding care and attention
and sometimes
even
neglect
with new shapes and interesting development.
So, I wonder about the two Pearls
and my family's image of them,
      dirt-stained hands,
      their marbly country voices,
      one hinting that sex was everything, overgrown
         and
      voluptuous,
      the other marrying for it, and then finding her
      husband, my cousin,
      would rather "bend his elbow" at the BPOE.

Plants come in, somehow,
when those other parts of sexual life fail.
I gratefully accept
that reality, knowing well how our bodies
fail us,
and wondering if my mother understands that her
failures have something to do
with her elderly house,
           empty of all plants, even
           African violets,

which she used to grow
so easily,
and which bloomed for her
practically untended,
while my Aunt Eva fumed and fussed
that hers
          (which by implication received meticulous care)
never got a bud on them.

Constantly juggling.
What we have.
What we don't have.
The pearls formed in my family out of irritation,
Family Jewels,
in a rugged Protestant world?

Saturday Night

for Barbara Drake

The muddy tangled week
was over
and Saturdays would be
late breakfast, a trip in the rattletrap Chevy to town
the weekly luxury of library,
department store,
shop windows,
and then supper out
and a movie.

We always had our supper at a sandwich shop
with polished formica counter and tables,
the soda machines gleaming stainless,
the shiny nozzles on the ice cream counter spotlessly
holding their chocolate, cherry, vanilla, coke
syrups.
We were usually there about 5 p.m.
when he had only a few customers, as he
closed at 6
on Saturdays.
Each week my mother would suggest I order something
different.
But I was firm,
what I wanted
never varied.
A ham sandwich on toasted bread with
mayonnaise served with potato chips and one slice of
        pickle
and a small coke. While my sister and
adventurous mother

would
each week
try little hamburgers,
bacon and tomato sandwiches
egg salad,
grilled cheese,
culinary explorers, never repeating, as
I,
unwaveringly,
ate my ham
sandwich,
drank my coke. After all,
for a child who drank a quart of milk a day,
scorned common (Wonder?) bread,
ate almost no sugar and whose
diet seldom contained any meat
but hamburger,
this seemed like
the most exotic meal in the world.

My favorite theater was The Whittier
on Whittier Blvd. It
had holes in the ceiling
which simulated stars.
The heavens twinkled as you watched
Betty Grable,
Gene Kelly,
Fred Astaire,
June Allyson,
my mother's favorites/ technicolor musicals.

What a feeling
coming home in darkness, Saturday nights,
having spent the day in town,
eaten my ham sandwich,

gone to the library,
gone window-shopping,
and seen the movie. Tucked on the floor of the car
beneath my feet
were my six library books, the limit allowed to each
person. Wealth,
rubies and diamonds, my week of reading,
though I would probably finish them all
by Monday.

I often fell asleep in the old car
as it travelled out of town
into the orange groves where we lived.
When we arrived
and my mother woke me up,
I would fuss to stay in the car all night.
I still think each morning
when I wake up and don't want to face the day
of how I felt then, not wanting to emerge
from the dusty old car,
wanting to snuggle down into the warm
backseat while it carried me through the night
of fragrant oranges,
a treasure of books at my feet
in a world where I could always be the princess,
never the servant,
never the poor peasant, living alone
in the country
with only an old mother.

White Gloves, White Feet

and we were on the subway,
the Kellys,
        Robert and Joby,
                and me,
going up to 125th St.
where we ate at a cheap Indian restaurant,
and I still wearing
my trunkfull of clothes from California
adolescence,
the full gathered skirt of thin
brown and white striped cotton voile
and its short-sleeved brown and white blouse;
I probably wore those patent leather shoes, flat heels,
    which
I used to wear
with grosgrain bows on them
flat and dancing-school-like,
(for Victorian girls)

and I also wore wrist length
white gloves,
not because New York was so dirty
—the summer so hot and all of us sweating
in the stuffy trains—
but because
a glove was something
to set me apart
from my mother
and Robert Kelly said to me,
        "Diane,
        do me a favor/ don't wear those gloves"

I took them off/ where are they now?

At the restaurant, we
all ordered curried meats; I
loved the lamb, vindaloo, as hot as you could get it,
and we ate paratha, and dahl, and our curries heaped on
    plates
and garnished with hot lime pickle, and spicy onion
    chutney,
green mango chutney for the real throatburner,
and when we were all finished and there were empty
    plates
all round, covered with gravy stains and some untidy
    heaps of
stained rice, Robert said,
        "Look at Diane's plate," and on it was a
    snowy white pile
of rice,
just as it had been served,
untouched by the juices, the meat curry and chutneys
    and pickles
eaten at the side, never having touched
the perfect white mound of rice.

I explained that I didn't eat starches but no one listened.
The pure white pile was more interesting itself
among the soiled dishes.

A last image: I had been in New York for seven months
    and it was spring,
time to put on sandals (at least the time for a Californian
to put them on)
standing outside the 10th St. Coffee House, talking to
    Howard Ant
about Robert Kelly's poetry and his power

and Howard looked down at my feet
which were glistening like ivory against the grimy
lower east side pavement,
                    "You must have the whitest
                              feet
in New York," he said with awe.

A few years later, having acquired a New Yorker's
        awareness of the
necessity of suntan (an awareness
I had never had in Southern California,
growing up there)
I would have been ashamed to appear in public
with such white feet. Almost like being bare breasted.

I blushed when Howard said that,
but when I got home my feet seemed very dirty
just from walking across town,
and I had my first inkling of the function
of a tan.

My hands, my feet, my concept of belly
all so white
in those days
                    memories of
wanting to
be
a princess.

SUMMER

Orphée

Eating Greek food,
grape leaves stuffed with rice and lamb,
moussaka with eggplant bursting out of nutmeg and
    oregano,
drinking retsina,
I think of my friend, Robert Kelly,
of my reluctance to control myself
and my anger at chaos.
Clint stands to my left,
Kelly on my right.
We each hold
scrupulous regard
for perfect food
and appropriate drink.
Victims of our bodies
we follow our imagination's exclusive
hunt
    Clint betrayed by the silver scissors of his lover,
    Kelly by himself, snipping whenever he can,
    and I, Atropos, the scissors, the mouth utters
    the syllables
    not wanting to control,
only mouthing,
a frame
to perfectly surround
a certain world,
and only the bather's foot
stepping onto the beach,
all else cut off.

Scissors,
framer,
each picture still.

And perfect.

Leaving Waterloo

It is dusk
and a mist is rising up from Bass Lake
just enough to make me realize
how hot the day has been
and how heated the shallow spots in the water have
    become,
the touch of visible breath
ensuing from cool night air moving over the day's
waters,
thinking of two long-dead people
I never met,
your grandparents, my ex-husband,
who in their old age,
after fifty years of marriage
sat in the same room with their backs turned to one
    another,
wishing their tiny house were two houses or
at least had enough room for
separate dwelling.

And how the old woman
refused
to be in the same hospital room
with her husband
when they were both taken sick
at once. The
anger and hatred those years had bred,
bees swarming in the old woman's head,
fire ants stinging her body,
a patch of nettles reddening her skin
at the very thought of the old man

whom she so thoroughly despised.
The story was a kind of joke
in your family,
Grandma with her chair turned to face the wall.
Yet,
I always winced when
I heard it,
and finally now
I'm grateful that you left me,
after only a few years
and me still crazy with salty love
for you.
I shudder
watching this evaporating dusk-lake water,
thinking of how
you could have turned your chair
to the wall in our house by the ocean,
simply refusing to speak to me for fifty years,
how easy it would have been for you,
how in keeping with the traditions
of your family.
Thank you for sparing me that horror,
the possibility that in anger
after looking at your turned back for years
I might have whirled you around only to find
the dead staring eye sockets of a skeleton,
faced with myself, as psycho-murderer,
not even knowing what I had done
to anger you so much,
still wondering what we inherit,
what we accept,
what traditions shape our lives.

Your grandmother turned in pain to face the wall
all those years?

Or was it only meanness?

Or something else? Was she trying to punish
fate, a simple old man,
for not being what she wanted or needed in her life?

I know you could have punished me that way
for all those things.
I am grateful, and thank you now,
for leaving. For not having
to watch you turn into your grandmother
sitting in her chair
facing the wall,
with your back forever to me.

The Frame

Choose any one.
It doesn't matter.
But let the window contain something
blue.
Let there be a receding horizon.
And an effect of skyline
along one edge.
If the blue were
a pool
and the man in short-sleeved shirt
skimming the water
with his long aluminum pole
and the day were thick with heat
and the brick walls were part of the horizon,
then the view would be this one
from out of my window,
the one I see now
remembering hot mornings
in the island of Hydra
when we would walk down the stone road
to the cafe
where cold silver packets of butter
would be served with our rolls,
and my morning tea
would never be hot enough.
Each morning
I would have the same
sense
this picture gives me
of beginning/ of a meal to be eaten/
never finished   NEVER left
with only crumbs and dirty cups and knives.

I would wish to have every
experience uncompleted
perfect
waiting
a meal about
to be consumed,
the painting showing
the man with his aluminum pole
ready to skim the clear turquoise pool water.
The frame enclosing the possibility of action,
retaining the scene.

Still.
Intact.

Eleanor on the Cliff

These houses along the empty cliff
are like old women in flowered cotton housecoats,
shabby, common, worn and
decent.
Before the real estate goldrush
these dry Southern hills,
thrusting up spiky yucca plants,
sloping towards Mexico,
held trailer parks and cheap houses,
orange and date stands,
poor people with a dry dream of freedom,
health nuts with a reptilian need
for sun.

As New Yorkers
who grew up in Brooklyn and The Bronx,
you found this shabby race-track town comfortable,
and moved with your infant son
into one of these old houses, crazed with unmended
    stucco walls,
right on a cliff over the beach,
the surf, the California ocean.
One day, on the patio,
which was cracked like an old woman's
    bunion-accommodated shoes,
I found you crying, Eleanor,
your still soft freckled face and dark hair
showing innocent pain.
"All my life," you said,
"I've wanted to live on the ocean,
in the sun,

the fresh air,
with a view like a postcard,
and now that I have it,
it's a nightmare. I am never sure
my son won't crawl or stumble over the cliff and kill
  himself,
it's lonely and miserable here,
and I can't drive, so I'm stuck
here all the time with the baby."

The purple ice plant
glowed against the lion yellow sandy cliffs.
It was one of those clear hot August days
with the sky, blue as an old man's washed and faded
  workshirt,
and I was trying to find the Golden things
on this beach that my birth had promised me.
Eleanor, my Eastern friend,
with her sense of humor
and unfailing urge for an interesting world,
who had husband and baby, house on the ocean,
  desirable loving life,
was weeping
in the sunshine,
telling me that realized dreams
become nightmares,
while I watched, as helpless as an old man who's had a
  stroke,
knowing all of her truth,
but my knowledge not preventing the truth
or even making the acceptance of it easier.

I thought of myself the year before,
lying in bed next to the woodsman,
telling him of my fear of trees,

that they are alive and move at night,
my fear of darkness,
the woods,
damp places,
his silence, my knowledge
at that moment
that I had said too much,
that is, disclosed something about myself
he would hold against me. The possibilities of betrayal
in our wishes, desires, and their
contradicting fears.
Each time I have had just
what I wanted,
I lost it or it went away. Still,
I know how getting what you want
can
turn into a nightmare,
Eleanor;
at that time I'd been spared for different troubles,
my own fantasies of perfection never realized for more
        than a few days
or weeks. But
I do know
how dream houses turn on people
and strangle them with ghost arms,
how jobs once longed for wrap us in shrouds of banality
        and boredom,
and even perfect lovers have such irritating habits
at the dinner table or snore so loud
you begin to wish you'd never married them.

How little in life
is satisfying,
except the unfulfilled urges, the
longing itself?

No lover was ever
what I'd hoped he'd be.
No friendship.
No child.
No job.
Certainly, no house.

Memory
has given me as much satisfaction
as longing, however.

These images:
        driving from Los Angeles to San Diego in
           1949,
        your cigarette-brown hills, Eleanor,
        rolling and empty as an old Camel pack,
        occasional glimpses of blue ocean as we
           dipped south
        past Capistrano,
        and finally came to sandy beaches.
        I wondered who bought the dates for sale
        at the orange juice stands,
        and why people would choose to live in a
           trailer.
        On those long rides I dreamed of the
           school boys I loved
        from behind my solemn little glasses.
        How surprised they
        would have been to see my
        pornographic dreams of love
        for their young healthy Southern
           California bodies.
        How could anybody's dream come true?

Yet, this memory I hold too:
of you crying,
that summer day in the patio,
the wide-brimmed hat you meticulously
    wore to keep sun
off your already freckled face, thrown
aside in distress,
the ocean pounding below us,
my ocean,
California's ocean,
which even here in the midwest
I hear pounding sometimes
at night.

Whole Sum

The swimming pool/ turquoise water
white rings of light undulating
on the surface,
each ring plunging down, rotating,
hula hoops of water-light appearing and disappearing
as the white-capped swimmers lap
the pool.

July
and I need to change my life
which tastes of shimmering red heaps of sliced
tomatoes
and translucent white slices of onion,
the picnic worship of salt,
the fruity granulation of sugared teeth.
Food in hampers,
sticky potato salad, tins of crisps,
buns, pickles which linger in vinegar,
cheeses which ferment and ripen in dark corners.

My vision of firm brown bodies,
curly heads,
shoulders dripping in jeweled elegance
from the swimming pool is this:
a frosty drink in hand,
the mouth ready for a summer feast.

Death,
disease, decay,
shoved into the mouth. Each bite
an attack on the liver. Each

sip an assault on the
kidney. Shovelling
picnic food into rubbery young bodies,
filling them with bites and
sips of death.
We are eating, eating
summer pleasure,
summer joy,
summer death.

We eat in communion with waste/ ALL we
eat is mud. The
swamp fills our mouth.

I sit this July morning
overlooking the turquoise water
undulating around the smooth brown swimmers.
They are fighting death,
while I walk willingly to my scrubbed
morning table,
willing to bite flaky croissants,
swallow gold butter,
taste a perfect egg (once a life's beginning),
drink mythic tea,
and know each beauty, each
pleasurable sensation
is my death.
My death from food,
as all death comes,
beautiful and terrible,
out of life.

Morning Thunderstorm

The fatigue of remaking
the world lies on the edge of my muscles
each morning
like an even film of dust on
shelves and furniture
created by a week's absence,
and I awake
with the pain of yesterday's food
decomposing inefficiently
in my body.
Morning offers me
another day in which to fail,
and a glimpse of tasks never to be accomplished,
no matter how much work is done.
                                        So it is pain
and fatigue
and a glimpse of the failing world
my own part in its failure
which makes me
hate the dawn;
and memories of my father's leaving
for his ship;
and lovers, dressing quietly in the dark
with no intention
of ever returning.
                        But this morning
I am awakened
by my favorite time of day—dusk.
Summer and seven a.m. (tho it feels p.m.),
the dark-sensitive ground-lamps have turned themselves
        on again,

the globes glowing steadily
against the grey Turner-esque sky.
The heat-lightning flickering on and off
as if a dozen news photographers were here
to document
this new day;
and the sound of thunder is,
in fact,
an old opening music which assures me of an elated
    night
with the orchestra.

Why do I get up so willingly this morning
almost in the dark
and go stand on my sultry porch beyond the
    air-conditioning,
feeling joy in this dark summer storm?
I, who love light but find dawn so painful a reminder
of rejection and failure?
Because the rain gives me that welcome feeling
of reaching the end of a long and meaningless journey?
While ordinary dawn only reminds me
of the daily labor required,
rolling the stone up the mountain,
and no change which can ever occur, no matter
the amount of labor. . .

Sailor's Daughter

for Edward Abbey

Each summer morning in Michigan
in my cool air-conditioned apartment
I pad around closing curtains
against heat and light,
then check each plant for moisture
        —the ferns always need a drink—
then, go out on my tiny balcony where the sun
is beating on my tomatoes,
and the sweet basil is pungently thrusting its fat leaves
    into the light.
I fill my watering cans several times. Drop
by drop, I water the babies just sprouting or the repotted
    anthuriums,
then deluge the sweet peas and marigolds.
The pansies (pensées) blink at me;
the Colorado Spruce,
a poor ragged thing, always slurps up a gallon or two.

And the first thing I drink (friends will tell you this)
                      each morning
is a goblet of icy tap water
with a golden slice of lemon floating
in it
and a sprig of fresh mint from
the porch garden.

This Westener who loves the desert,
loves water more. Yet, I too, Mr. Abbey,
appreciate those stoney, bare
waterless islands,

111

and the miles and miles of alkali wastes.
Perhaps that is where I learned the preciousness of
    language,
each word, a drop, refreshing silence;

I, daughter of a pillar of salt,
lamenting a past I never had;
I, sailor's daughter, afraid of water, parched,
burnishing her salty, salty tongue.

Peaches

Soft baskets full of their yielding flesh
ripening at once
overwhelmingly
the sugar bleeding from spots where the skin
slides away.
This mid-summer luxuriance
falling somewhere
in muffled thuds from the trees,
the small scimitar-shaped leaves cling to a few stems
like green mustaches.

Somewhere in California
my blood line goes on,
making me unnecessary.
I'm just another soft peach
which should quickly be preserved
or eaten
in the cool morning,
the sticky juice
making each finger
momentarily fragrant.

                 My silence means
nothing
or so many things,
one cannot take it
                 personally.

Gardenias

for Norman Hindley

Norman, this summer
just as you left the lush swamp of Michigan, wearing
your Cap of Darkness jacket
and carrying your tarragon mustard and
the feather-light tin of husk-dry green peppercorns,
my potted gardenia
which had been sweating and covering itself
with buds, furled and wound tight like turbans,
began to bloom.
        You, who gave me
the weekly gift of gardenias
when we lived on Molokai
fired me with the desire to make my own white flowers
show their morning radiance,
and jasmine the Michigan night with their scent.
But my apartment, always too dry and cool/
so, in their little tub they were given to the outdoor
    balcony and the
real nights
and days of midwest summer.
Did you know that when each flower blooms
it opens one petal at a time
like the hands of a clock,
moving,
slowly
towards 12. Sometimes the opening seemed slower than
    it was;
I, used to the surprise of a plant suddenly
burst into bloom,
flowers at once

where previously there was nothing or only
the hidden.
But, each gardenia
opens almost exactly like the
clock it emulates,
one petal, one hour, a second, a third,
from morning when there were only stripes of white, till
    evening
when the whole wedding dress flower has extended its
    toothy petals.

On Molokai, we
didn't have a Christmas tree
because they cost $50 apiece,
and besides it seemed bizarre and ugly
to be in a tropical land celebrating a season
which doesn't exist there.
Your son, Christopher, said to us
when he heard we had no Christmas tree,
"You mean you'll wake up Christmas morning and there
    will only be
beer and wine bottles
on your living room floor?"

No, there were gardenias too,
and the magnificent bird's-nest fern
you lent us for our stay.
But most of all, there was the promise
of our friendship,
of the celebration at your house
where the big gardenia bush grows.
The roast beef grilled to rare succulence,
the room full of Pamela's beautiful paintings,
and the unimportant Christmas tree and presents.

Now, we've celebrated mid-Summer together too.
With wine and poetry and more roast beef.
On your departure,
gardenias replace you in our living room.
Friendship,
not just of holidays,
but for all seasons.

For Clint on the Desert

This morning folds me
into a breast pocket, like a ticket,
in a wallet,
and the rain is a medium of travel. On it
I go to Manhattan 15 years
ago,
walking in the rain in the fashionable
east sixties,
up from the Beekman Tower,
walking into a delicatessen with that unique smell
of refrigerated potato salad,
expensive lox,
cream cheese in flat stainless steel pans,
some with chives,
and the olives, big and black, heaped
next to it. Somehow the smell of
vinegar and coffee mingling
to prevent any olfactory pleasure.

Rain,
when I watched the evening traffic form
and knew my husband, at 21,
was already sleeping with other women,
and the rain
let the lights of the city traffic, looked down upon
from the 12th floor,
seem shinier
and life more inexorable, visible,
physical.
             Past longing
for the Pony Express

and its rider, the first mailman, I wanted
myself,
I suppose. Yet
could only think of sex.

How I want life to deliver me from
that body I saw
looking down on Manhattan traffic that
rainy dusk,
the lighted moving cars
which, each one, propelled bodies
that seem to me
insignificant, flickering like fireflies I see now
each summer evening in this
Michigan swamp.
Flickering among cattails,
not believable even, more like
a disturbance in the eye.
Darwin says,
writing in his journal while voyaging on *The Beagle:*

> *At these times the fireflies are seen flitting from*
> *hedge to hedge. On a dark night the light can be*
> *seen at about two hundred paces distant. . . I*
> *found that this insect emitted the most brilliant*
> *flashes when irritated: in the intervals, the*
> *abdominal rings were obscured. The flash was*
> *almost co-instantaneous in the two rings, but it*
> *was just perceptible first in the anterior one. The*
> *shining matter was fluid and very adhesive: little*
> *spots where the skin had been torn, continued*
> *bright with a slight scintillation, whilst the*
> *uninjured parts were obscured. When the insect*
> *was decapitated the rings remained*
> *uninterruptedly bright, but not so brilliant as*

before: local irritation with a needle always increased the vividness of the light. The rings in one instance retained their luminous property nearly twenty-four hours after the death of the insect. From these facts it would appear probable that the insect has only the power of concealing or extinguishing light for short intervals, and that at other times the display is involuntary.

ENVOI

A Letter to Wang Wei
on the Season of Tumultuous Magicians

I.
His name is the smoke exhaust
of a motorcycle.
His hand shoots a flame at me
when I open the door.
I ask him to pick a card,
any card,
and he always comes up with my photograph,
tho I was never royalty
nor did my face show
when he shuffled
but time and again
when I did not see him
his hat was left
on my bed,
and I knew he loved me
even tho he
was invisible.

II.
This one used mirrors.
I kept thinking
someday
a mirror would shatter.
But the glass remained whole
as pear
or a snake.
I would never find him
tho I looked beyond my own image for even a
shadow which might

independently move.
"I love you,"
I called to the magician,
the one man
who had many shapes.
"I love you," I called,
shivering in cold mirrors,
hearing doors slam in the background,
occasionally finding an empty hat
left on my bed.
But his mirrors
which yielded
many other illusions
never reflected him.

The hat was empty for many years on my bed. At last
I am studying
the art of conjuring.
Perhaps
you will see me soon
walking down the street with that strong face
I love so much,
his hat on his head,
and our mouths smiling and flashing
like mirrors.
                    Love,
you magician,
lend me
your books. I must learn from the past.

III.
This one was strong and substantial with shoulders like
        a bull.
But he too could
disappear.

When I said,
"I love you,"
he began to fade,
> first his mustache
> then his silky hair
> his powerful shoulders thinning
> and disappearing
> as a . . .
But I learned another magic,
the art of silence.
And now my magician is with me,
strong and beautiful.
No words pass my lips, but silence is joyful
like a hawk circling over the mountain on a clear day.
I am silent,
and my magician stands by me.
Performing illusions for the world,
swallowing flames,
untying my silk scarves,
sawing beautiful women in half.
> Love,
you are some silent speaker
in my wilderness.

Why I Am Not a Painter

*with thanks to Frank O'Hara, as I
borrowed his title*

(For years I have been troubled by a very strong intuitive
response to natural landscape. It is a double response, for
I *do* see the scene I am looking at as a painting, one
already painted, and at the same time, I involuntarily
think, and feel a strong emotion as I am thinking this, "I
wish I were a painter.")

No ideas
but in things? But then,
why do I want
to paint this world today? A thaw in our
egret landscape
and then fast freeze,
this morning
each tree etched with frost.
My holly plant
sitting on the steps in its inadequate pot
shows each leaf outlined in crystal
and the bare
forsythia bushes wave thin ice-crusted
twigs. What ideas come to me
seeing this world?
None.
But I want to paint it, so I call home
after a walk to my office
and tell my husband
he should photograph it.
              Why?
Too easy to say

it won't be that way tomorrow. If I
wanted to hold the image,
why didn't I stay outdoors
looking at it all day? I had
nothing
better to do. But I went inside and buried myself
in a book.
This
has been true
each time
I have seen something
I wanted to paint:
>the plantation oaks on Jekyl Island,
>the curving cliffs at Laguna Beach,
>the fog canyons,
>autumn in the Blue Ridge Mountains,
I almost get shorthand messages now
from my brain/ "I wish I were a painter. I'd paint this
>scene."
and "Therefore you don't need to look at it very long."

Do I want to paint it because that
would force me to set up my easel
and sit for a long time looking at the scene?
Why don't I simply sit and look at something I find
>beautiful?

What does beauty in my eye
do to me?
>The carbon cave
>soots my eyes. Oh, John Dunn, my
>>ophthalmologist,
>surely you represent
>clear vision.
>What else is poetry? But looking down

the labyrinth to a California past
shows me the darkness of sex.
Is it possible
to plant a garden
and not see the ground open up?
The wasp which has been flying around in my
    bedroom
now clings to the window's cold,
scarcely moves, but in the ground
swollen with white kernel
is an old civilization.

I am looking at some cuttings of a
velvet plant, in a fat green bottle
which once held framboise.
Their curving leaves, like arrowheads,
are glowing magenta in the afternoon sun, their
delicate princess hair roots, fine and white,
almost filling the bottle, beginning
to curl around its bottom.

The glow of the soft leaves
reminds me of all the beauty I would like to paint.
How much I prefer a tree, this huge fig plant,
a night-blooming cereus which has never bloomed
reaching long fleshy fingers into today's sunshine, the
bristly spruces with each clump of needles
outlined by ice.

The human form is one I wish I did not possess.
    Daphne, you were not punished.
    Narcissus, none of you.
    How much I would rather be
    a plant
    than what I am.

Is this why I wish I were a painter?
For it is a painter of landscapes
and of still lives I would be.
Humans and animals
so trivial, uninteresting. But water lilies,
yes, or Stevens' "junipers shagged with ice."
Does this explain why
some few
of us
who live in apartments
read the Burpee and other seed
catalogues?
Or why I, who once cared everything
for egg beauty
and the passionate life
now prefer
still lives,
the bloom of plant life
a world where desire has been eliminated?

Printed February 1982 in Santa Barbara & Ann Arbor
for the Black Sparrow Press by Graham Mackintosh
& Edwards Brothers Inc. Design by Barbara Martin.
This edition is published in paper wrappers;
there are 750 hardcover trade copies; 250 copies
have been numbered & signed by the author; &
50 numbered copies have been handbound in boards
by Earle Gray each containing an original holograph
poem by Diane Wakoski.

Diane Wakoski has published 13 collections of poems, one collection of essays, and many slim volumes of poetry. She serves part of each year as Writer in Residence at Michigan State University. Most of the important facts concerning her life can be found in her poems.

Photo: Robert Turney